W9-AYO-678

Pitt Street PIRATES

by Terry Deary

illustrated by Steve Donald

*Cover illustration by
Brett Hawkins*

Librarian Reviewer
Laurie K. Holland
Media Specialist (National Board Certified), Edina, MN
MA in Elementary Education, Minnesota State University, Mankato, MN

Reading Consultant
Elizabeth Stedem
Educator/Consultant, Colorado Springs, CO
MA in Elementary Education, University of Denver, CO

STONE ARCH BOOKS
Minneapolis   San Diego

First published in the United States in 2006
by Stone Arch Books,
151 Good Counsel Drive, P.O. Box 669,
Mankato, Minnesota 56002.
www.stonearchbooks.com

Published by arrangement with
Barrington Stoke Ltd, Edinburgh.

Library of Congress Cataloging-in-Publication Data
Deary, Terry.
   Pitt Street pirates / by Terry Deary; illustrated by Steve Donald.
   p. cm. — (Pathway Books.)
   Summary: While trying to beat their town's rich kids in a treasure hunt,
Captain Roger Redbeard, Sniffles the cabin boy, and Ellie, a band of modern-
day pirates, uncover a real treasure.
   ISBN-13: 978-1-59889-005-1 (hardcover)
   ISBN-10: 1-59889-005-0 (hardcover)
   ISBN-13: 978-1-59889-197-3 (paperback)
   ISBN-10: 1-59889-197-9 (paperback)
   [1. Pirates—Fiction. 2. Buried treasure—Fiction. 3. Humorous stories.]
I. Donald, Steve, ill. II. Title. III. Series.
PZ7.D3517Pit 2006
[Fic]—dc22   2005026581

1 2 3 4 5 6 11 10 09 08 07 06

Printed in the United States of America.

TABLE OF CONTENTS

CAST OF CHARACTERS

Captain of the Pitt Street Pirates and master shipbuilder, Roger calls himself Redbeard, but he doesn't even have a beard! In fact, he's too young to shave, and he never washes behind his ears.

Roger

Minnie's the ship's parrot, and the only four-legged parrot on Pitt Street.

Minnie

She's not as tall as a gorilla, nor as pretty, but a lot stronger. Ellie has only two weaknesses — chocolate and Roger Redbeard.

Ellie

The weak and skinny member of the gang, Sniffle has all the brains of a tin can — an empty tin can that is.

Sniffle

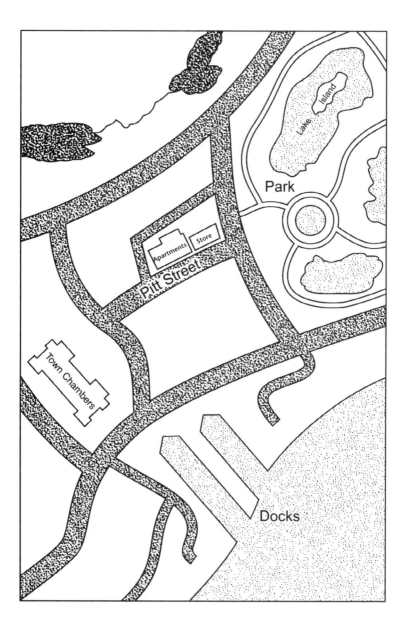

Chapter 1

A PITT STREET PLAN

Roger Redbeard did not have a red beard.

"Why are you called Redbeard?" Sniffle Smith, his skinny friend, wanted to know.

"Because my family is called Redbeard," Roger told him. "Why are you called Sniffle?"

"Don't know," Sniffle sniffed. "Was your dad called Redbeard?"

Roger put a hand on his thick, black hair. "I never met my dad," he said.

"So does your mom have a red beard?" Sniffle asked.

Roger gave a sigh. Sniffle was as dumb as they come. "The Redbeards took their name from Captain Redbeard. He was a great pirate!" Roger said with pride.

"What sort of planes did he fly?" Sniffle asked.

"P-I-R-A-T-E. Pirate, you goof! Not pilot!" Roger said. "The terror of the high seas! Robber of Spanish gold!"

Sniffle gave a sigh. "I wish we were pirates. I'd like to find some gold."

"Why not, Sniffle? Why don't we do that?" Roger wanted to know.

Roger looked hard at the old houses across the street. He closed his eyes and saw them in his mind as galleons — great ships under full sail.

"Er, is it because we haven't got a ship?" Sniffle asked.

"We'll build one! Mr. Clark at the corner store has stacks of old wooden boxes! We'll build a ship and sail the seven seas."

"But I have to be back in time for supper," Sniffle said.

"Then we'll sail the seven park lakes!" Roger shouted and jumped to his feet.

He ran down the street to the corner store. Sniffle walked slowly after him.

Out of a dark corner came Minnie, a skinny, flea-bitten cat.

* * *

Roger Redbeard was the first of his family in 400 years to build a pirate ship. And the first one ever to build it in his backyard. Sniffle sniffed when he saw it.

"It'll never float!" Sniffle exclaimed.

"Ha! That's what they said about the *Titanic*!" Roger said with a grin.

"Did they?" asked Sniffle.

"They did! And look where the *Titanic* ended up!" he said.

"I see!" Sniffle smiled, but he didn't see. He still felt unhappy.

"Can I be the captain?" he asked.

"You can be the cabin boy," Roger told him. "You can go up into the crow's nest and keep a look out."

"Is that a big job?"

"You can't get any higher," Roger grinned.

After hours of hard work, the boat was ready. There were just one or two problems.

"How do we get it down to the lake?" asked Sniffle.

"What a stupid thing to ask," Roger replied. "How do they get a ship in a bottle?"

"I don't know," said Sniffle.

"Well, there you are!" Roger cried.

"But it won't fit through the gate!"

"It came in the gate, didn't it?" Roger grinned again.

But Sniffle was right.

"Push!" the captain told him. Sniffle pushed. The boat didn't move.

"You push, and I'll pull!" Roger said.

The cabin boy pushed one end, and the captain pulled the same end. The boat didn't move. Captain Redbeard stroked his beardless chin.

"We need more help," he said. "And I know just where to get it!"

Roger ran up the steps of the building and then down the hall to apartment 13.

Chapter 2

A MIGHTY MATE

In apartment 13, Ellie was lying on her bed. It was a huge bed. Ellie was a big girl. She was reading a book and watching an old black-and-white movie. She was clever like that. She could do two things at once.

Sniffle could never do two things at once.

Ellie heard a knock at the door. "Come in!" she called.

Roger kicked the door open. CRACK!

"Roger!" Ellie cried and gave him a hug. "You don't know how long I've waited for this moment," she sighed.

"What moment?" Roger blinked.

"Why, the moment when you walked in here just to see me. What do you want?" she asked gently.

"He wants to fish," Sniffle said.

"I'm Captain Roger Redbeard, and I need help getting my new ship into the water," he told her.

Ellie jumped off the bed. "Oh, are you playing pirates? Can I join the crew?"

"Not playing," Roger said. "And there aren't women pirates."

"Yes, there are. There's one in the opera *The Pirates of Penzance*. She's called Ruth," Ellie said.

"Well," Roger said, "my crew of pirates is going to be Ruth-less. Hee! Hee! Hee! Get it? Ruth-less!"

Sniffle smiled. But he didn't get the joke.

"Okay, but then you don't get the boat in the water," said Ellie with a shrug.

"You're in the crew," Roger said quickly. "First Mate Ellie."

"She could have my job in the cow's nest," Sniffle offered.

"Crow's nest," Roger hissed.

"Whatever you say," said Sniffle.

Ellie led the way to the door. "Avast and belay there!" she cried. (She'd read the right pirate books.)

"Er, how do I do that?" Sniffle asked.

Roger gave a shrug and went into the backyard with Ellie.

Ellie looked at the ship. "It'll never float," she said sadly.

Sniffle smiled. What had Roger told him? "That's what they said about the *Titanic*! And look where it ended up!"

"At the bottom of the sea," said Ellie. "It hit an iceberg."

There was no reply to that. Sniffle sniffed.

Sniff. Sniff!

Roger looked at her. He was angry.

"Are you going to say it won't go through the gate?" he snapped.

"Yeah," the cabin boy cut in. "Well, how do they get bottles in ships?"

Ellie smiled. "Never mind. It can go over the wall." And she picked up the galleon and carried it toward the street. Roger put a hand under the ship. "Okay, Ellie, I've got it!"

Ellie lifted the ship onto the top of the wall and ran through the gate to catch it as it slid into the back alley. Then she marched off toward Pitt Street Park. The captain, the cabin boy, and the skinny cat ran after her.

Small kids rushed to their doors to look at the strange sight — a galleon in full sail moving down Pitt Street!

"What are you calling the ship, Roger?" Mr. Clark called out as the ship passed the corner store.

Roger thought fast. "Er, the *Titanic*!" he called.

Old Mr. Clark shook his head. "Hope there are no icebergs down on the park lake."

There were no icebergs. But there were lots of kids with sailboats and motorboats of all shapes and sizes. When the Pitt Street Pirates and the *Titanic* got to the edge of the lake, the kids ran away to hide in the bushes as if they'd seen a mad dog. Soon the lake was empty. Ellie slid the ship onto the grass at the edge of the lake.

"How's that, Captain?" she asked.

Roger gave a shrug. "Not bad. But you didn't have to carry it the whole way. Sniffle and I could have done it on our own, you know."

"Aye, aye, Captain," Ellie said in a humble voice.

Roger Redbeard patted his good ship with pride. "I name this ship *Titanic*."

"May God bless her and all who sail in her," Ellie added.

"I was just going to say that," Roger snapped. "May dogs dress her and all who fail in her!"

He gave the ship a big push to send her sliding into the cruel sea.

Sniffle cheered. Minnie the cat purred. Ellie clapped.

But the *Titanic* didn't budge.

Chapter 3

A TREASURE ISLAND

Fifty kids were watching from the bushes in Pitt Street Park as Ellie stepped up to the galleon and pushed it gently toward the water. Fifty kids were silent as the *Titanic* hit the water with a splash. Fifty kids and Ellie and a cat gasped as the ship bobbed happily up and down on the water.

"It floats!" Ellie shouted.

Roger gave a shrug and tried not to look too pleased.

"What did you think it would do?" he asked.

"Float, Captain," said Ellie, grinning. "Shiver me timbers."

"Er, shiver your what?" asked Roger.

"Me timbers, Captain. That's what all the pirates say," Ellie told him.

"Do they?" Roger blinked. "You seem to know a lot about pirates."

"I've read all the books and seen all the movies. I know all about them!" she told him.

"Uh-huh. Anything else you think I should know about them?" Roger asked.

"Don't worry. I'll tell you everything in the pirates' den tonight."

"Pirates' den?" Sniffle cut in.

"That's right! My room," Ellie went on happily. "Ship's biscuits and grog!"

"I don't like frogs," Sniffle said.

Roger just shook his head. This pirate stuff was a lot harder than he thought.

"All aboard the *Titanic*!" he cried as he stepped off the shore and onto the swaying ship.

Sniffle followed. He had a hard time getting up to the crow's nest at the top of the mast. The mast was weak, and it swayed slightly.

The ship sank a little lower in the water as Ellie got in with a cry of "Shiver me timbers!"

Minnie the cat jumped on board just as Ellie pushed them into the lake.

Roger grabbed the rudder and tried to steer. He closed his eyes. Now he could see the seven seas ahead of them.

"Tiver me shimbers!" he yelled. He looked up to the top of the mast.

"Can you see anything, Mr. Cabin Boy?" he cried.

Sniffle pointed back to the shore.

"A Spanish galleon, Captain!" he called back.

Roger swung around. On the shore, a little girl stood and glared at them. She wore the frilliest, whitest dress Roger had ever seen.

"Hey! You people in that boat! Come here at once!" she ordered.

"Turn the ship around, and go back, Ellie!" Roger said.

"You mean avast and belay, don't you?" the first mate asked.

"Do I?" replied the dazed captain.

"Aye, aye, Sir!" Ellie cried and paddled back to shore.

Roger stared at the little girl. She had small blue bows in her hair, but he wasn't looking at her hair. He was looking at her tricycle. It was a three-wheeler, and it glittered like a galleon full of gold.

The *Titanic* bumped up against the shore, and Sniffle fell into the lake.

"Help! Roger! Help! I can't swim. Help! I'm drowning!" he wailed.

"No, you're not," Ellie said with a sigh. "The water's only up to your knees. Stand up, Cabin Boy."

Sniffle gave a silly grin. He was soaking wet as he got out of the lake.

"Now," the girl on the golden tricycle said, "I want you to take me out to the island in the middle of the lake."

Roger just gazed at her, and Sniffle just grinned. Ellie looked angry. "Why should we?" she asked.

The little girl tossed her curls and said, "Because I'm Ruby Rose."

"I'm sorry to hear that," Sniffle said.

"My daddy is the mayor, Mayor Rupert Rose," Ruby went on. "The country club is having a Fun Day."

"It's my job to organize the town treasure hunt," she added.

"Treasure!" said Roger, excitedly.

"I plan to hide a clue on that island in the lake," Ruby told them. "So take me across in that raft of yours."

"Yes, Miss," Roger said.

"No way," Ellie snapped.

"Wait a moment," said Roger to Ellie. "I'm the captain."

"Sorry, Sir," Ellie said in a low voice. "But we can make some money out of this. She'll have to pay us!"

Roger looked excited. "Yeah!" he said to Ruby. "It'll cost you ten cents."

"A dollar!" Ellie said.

"Okay," Ruby Rose agreed.

"I'll pay you your money when we're safely back," Rose added.

They set off across the lake again with Miss Ruby Rose aboard. The Pitt Street Pirates sailed in silence. They had to. Ruby talked so much.

"This will be the next to the last clue. If people solve this one, they'll find the clue that tells them where the treasure is," she told them.

She pulled a slip of paper from her frilly, white bag and held it under Roger's nose. It said:

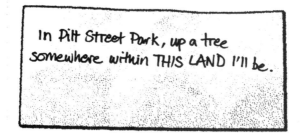

In Pitt Street Park, up a tree somewhere within THIS LAND I'll be.

"Get it?" Ruby asked with a grin.

Roger shook his head.

"Good!" said Ruby. "Only the really brainy ones will get the answer."

"Can I look?" Ellie asked. Ellie looked at the paper. "Easy," she said.

Ruby's face turned an angry red. "No, it's not! There are hundreds of trees in Pitt Street Park."

"But only one on the island," Ellie said softly.

"How do you know it's on the island?" asked Ruby angrily.

"The clue says, 'Somewhere within THIS LAND.' Take the I-S from THIS and the L-A-N-D, and you have I-S-L-A-N-D. Island!"

"Land ahoy!" Sniffle cried.

"You only knew that because that's where we're going," said Ruby

"Land a-HOYYYY!" Sniffle yelled.

"Oh no, I didn't!" Ellie said sharply.

"Oh yes, you did!"

"Land a-HOYYYY!!" yelled Sniffle.

"Oh no, I didn't!"

"Oh yes, you — eeeeek!"

CCCRRRUUNNCCCHH!!!

The *Titanic* hit the island.

"Land a-help!" Sniffle cried as he flew from the crow's nest and landed in the island's only tree.

"Abandon ship!" Roger cried as he climbed ashore.

"My daddy will have you punished!" Ruby cried as green water lapped over her shiny red shoes.

"Sorry, Captain," Ellie said with a sheepish smile as the *Titanic* sank in the shallow water.

Chapter 4

A FOUR-LEGGED PARROT

Ellie lifted Sniffle down from the tree. Then Ruby gave her the treasure hunt clue. "Put that up in the tree!" she ordered.

This time Ellie didn't argue with her. Ellie reached up as high as she could and placed the clue in the tree.

Sniffle was taking twigs out of his nose. "How do we get back, Captain Roger?" he asked.

Roger was looking at the huge hole in the *Titanic*'s side.

"Swim," he said.

"I can't swim!" Sniffle told him.

"And I won't!" Ruby said and stamped her slimy sock. "I'll just wait here until Daddy's helicopter comes to rescue me. And you'll have to pay for the gas," she warned.

"I guess I'll have to carry you back," Ellie said. "The water's not too deep for me."

So Ellie carried Ruby over to the shore, and Roger carried Sniffle. Minnie sat on Sniffle's head.

"Don't splash that smelly water on my dress!" Ruby said. "It cost 1,000 dollars in Paris!"

"And I don't think much of your outfit, dear Ellie!" said Ruby. "It's only good to clean floors with."

When Ellie got to the shore, Ruby ordered, "Put me down."

Ellie turned and walked back to the edge of the lake. She dropped Ruby into the water. Ruby landed in the weediest part of the lake.

Ruby came up spitting out tadpoles.

"You'll be hearing from my daddy!" Ruby yelled as the Pitt Street Pirates ran off. They could hear Ruby wailing as she got on her tricycle. "Oh, no! Someone's stolen my hubcaps!"

Roger panted as they ran, "We didn't get our money from her."

Ellie grinned. "Never mind. I've got something much better!" She opened her fist and waved a slip of paper under Roger's nose. "I've got the last clue to the treasure hunt. If we solve the clue, we get the prize! So meet me tonight in the pirates' den!"

* * *

Later that evening, Ellie switched off her TV and smiled. "That pirate in the movie was doing just what pirates have to do!" she said.

"Just like my Auntie Jane," Sniffle said.

"Is your Auntie Jane a pirate?"

"No, but she does what she has to do."

"Quiet, Sniffle," Roger sighed.

"Yes, Captain Roger," said Sniffle.

"And what was that song again, me hearty?" Captain Redbeard asked.

"Fifteen men on the dead man's chest, Yo-ho-ho . . ." Ellie sang.

Sniffle shook his head. "That song's no good for me, Captain."

"Why not?" asked Roger.

"I can't count up to 15. I only have ten fingers."

"You land blubber," Roger snarled.

"Lubber!" Ellie said. "Land lubber."

"Yeah!" Roger nodded. "He's one of those, too. I'll soon have you talking to tanks!"

"Walking the plank," Ellie corrected.

"Yeah, that's it! Walking the plank!" Captain Redbeard turned to Ellie. "Am I starting to sound like a real pirate?" he asked.

"Oh, much better," she smiled. "And, of course, you're better looking!"

"Of course," Roger agreed.

"Now all we need are pirate clothes," she went on. "I've made scarves for Sniffle and me."

Sniffle sniffed with joy as he saw the bright red silk scarves.

"Where did you get the silk?" he gasped.

"Mom's scarves," she said.

"Won't she miss them?"

"Not until it gets colder," said Ellie.

"I'm not wearing them on my head," Roger said.

"Oh, no," Ellie told him sweetly. "I made this for you." And she pulled out a black pirate hat that fit Roger's head. "Now you're a real pirate captain," she said.

"Yeah!" Captain Redbeard said as he looked at himself with pride in the cracked mirror.

He undid his shirt to the waist, kicked off his shoes, and strutted up and down the room. "Are we all ready to go now?"

Ellie shook her head. "You need a parrot."

"Where will we find a parrot around Pitt Street?" Sniffle asked.

Ellie looked at Minnie the cat.

All at once, Ellie's long arm shot out, and she grabbed the cat. With her other hand, she tied a string around Minnie's head and clamped a beak made of cardboard onto her nose. She put the puzzled cat on Roger's shoulder.

"Now we are a pirate crew!" she said.

"Yeah, but without a ship," Sniffle pointed out.

"Ah, but with a treasure chest to find," she said. "Let's figure out this last clue to Ruby Rose's treasure hunt. We'll be able to buy 100 ships by this time tomorrow," she told them.

The treasure is there
if you seek deep down
in the jumbled EARTH
of the MATCHES BROWN

Chapter 5

THE CROOKED COW

"I'll read the clue," Ellie said.

She unfolded the grubby slip of paper that Ruby had given her to put up in the tree.

"That's it!" Roger cried. "It says 'matches brown.' The matches you can buy in Brown's store. Do you think that's it?"

"I don't think so," Ellie told him.

But Roger just kept on talking. "Do you know any stores owned by a Mr. or Mrs. Brown?" he asked Sniffle.

Sniffle blinked. "Old Buddy Brown runs the Crooked Cow on Dock Street."

Roger punched the air. "That's it!" Then he punched his cabin boy on the arm. "Well done, Sniffle! Well done! Maybe you're not as stupid as you look."

Roger jumped to his feet.

"We just have to dig behind the Crooked Cow!" he said.

"No!" Ellie said. "You don't understand . . ."

"Hey!" Sniffle looked scared. "That's a scary old place!"

"They say that Baby Face Ging, the master criminal from England, used to hang out there with his gang," Sniffle added.

Roger walked toward the door with Minnie on his shoulder. Ellie grabbed Sniffle's hand and ran after them.

"Why would Ruby Rose want to hide treasure there?" she asked.

Roger grabbed a shovel as he rushed out into the cool, night air.

"The clue is jumbled in the word, Roger!" Ellie tried to tell him. "It means the letters are all mixed up to make another word."

But Roger didn't listen to her. He ran down the dark street with his crew following him.

"You see," Ellie was saying, "mix up the letters in BROWN MATCHES to make new words, and you get TOWN CHAMBERS."

"That's where the Town Council meets," she explained. "That's where a girl like Ruby Rose would hide the treasure. You understand, Sniffle, don't you?"

"Er, no, Ellie," Sniffle replied.

Ellie went on. "The letters E-A-R-T-H can be changed to make HEART. And the letters in B-R-O-W-N M-A-T-C-H-E-S make TOWN CHAMBERS. See?"

"Er, no, Ellie," Sniffle said.

"The treasure's in the Town Chambers!" she told them. "The Town Hall!"

Sniffle shook his head.

"Captain Roger was right about the *Titanic,*" he told her. "So he'll be right this time, too."

"Yes," she said. "He's a great captain and a fantastic shipbuilder, but he's no good at word games!"

Roger rushed on down the dark streets muttering, "Avast and belay there, me hearties. Pieces of eight and Spanish gold!"

The tooting of the tugboats broke the silence of the dark streets as the kids came near the old dock area of the town.

The cool, damp river air made Ellie shiver.

The shapes in the shadows made Sniffle shake.

But bold Roger Redbeard raced on with dreams of gold to keep out the cold.

At last he got to the back wall of the Crooked Cow.

Chapter 6

HELLO ELLO

Minnie the cat fell off his shoulder as Roger tried to scramble up the high brick wall. Ellie came after him.

"Let me help you, Captain!" she said.

She cupped her hands, Roger put one foot in them, and she lifted him up a little too fast. Roger shot over the wall like a cannonball and landed in the yard on his head.

He shook himself. He could hear faint sounds of laughter spilling out from the Crooked Cow. A tomcat howled close by. Minnie, the ship's parrot, howled back.

Closer still, someone moved in the shadows by the gate.

"Who's that?" the bold pirate captain whispered.

"Who's that?" said a shaky voice.

"Who's that, saying, 'Who's that?'" replied Roger.

"Who's that, saying, 'Who's that, saying, who's that?'" the shaky voice shook.

"I asked first," Roger Redbeard said. "Who are you?"

"Not telling," sniffed the voice.

"Sniffle?" Roger said. "How did you get in here?"

"By the gate," the cabin boy replied. "It was open, you know."

Roger gave a sigh. A pirate's life is never easy.

"Let Ellie in," he ordered.

Then he began digging away at the hard dirt in the corner of the yard.

"You two find your own patch and let me know if you find anything."

After half an hour Roger was up to his neck in a hole. He hit solid rock. He looked out. He felt stiff. The yard was silent.

"Ellie?" he asked.

"Aye aye, Captain?"

"Found anything?" he asked.

"Twenty-three worms and six dog bones," Ellie replied

"Sniffle?"

"Sniff?" sniffed Sniffle.

"Found anything?" Roger asked.

"Nah. Just an old brown suitcase."

"A brown suitcase!" the captain cried. "What's in it? Gold, silver, and jewels?"

"No. Nothing like that. It's full of paper. Looks like paper money!"

"Treasure!" Ellie and the captain cried at once.

They slammed the case shut and rushed out into the alley.

They also rushed into the arms of a police officer.

"Now, what have we got here?" Officer Ello asked. He took the case from the captain's hands. "Had a report of noises in the backyard of the Crooked Cow. The owner was worried! I came around to see what was going on. You kids should be in bed at this time of night."

The police officer pressed the catch on the case. Its lid sprang open. Piles of paper money fell out. The police officer looked amazed. "And where did you get all this money?"

"Behind the Crooked Cow," Ellie said sadly. "Roger guessed that it would be there."

"Did he now?" the police officer grinned. "Well, he's more clever than all the town's police! People have been looking for Baby Face Ging's loot for 25 years and have never found it."

"This is Ruby Rose's treasure hunt prize," Sniffle said.

Officer Ello smiled. "Nah! That's in the heart of the Town Chambers. Everyone knows that! No, this is Baby Face Ging's treasure, stolen from the Bank of England. This money is all in English pounds, not dollar bills. And you found it. You know what that means?"

Roger gave a sigh. He was worn out. It had been a bad day. "Bad news," was all he could say.

"Ha! No! More like a reward!" the police officer grinned. "I'll just look after the money for you. It's old and probably not worth anything."

"Come to the Town Chambers tomorrow. I bet the mayor will have a big reward for you," he said.

The police officer stuffed the money back in the case, picked it up, and plodded off down the back alley.

The pale street lamps gleamed in Ellie's eyes. "Oh, Roger," she said. "You are wonderful!"

Even in the dark, Roger's cheeks glowed red.

"Avast, me hearties!" he roared. "We'll meet tomorrow in the Town Chambers!"

Chapter 7

PAPER TREASURE

Mayor Rupert Rose blinked and put on his glasses. "Now that the Town Council's work is done," he said, "I can present the prizes to the finders of the treasure!"

He took an envelope out of his pocket. "In this envelope there are two tickets for a tropical island vacation."

"Oh, Roger," Ellie crooned. "You and I can go away together."

The pirate captain looked a little unhappy. "Wouldn't you rather take Sniffle?" he asked. Ellie punched him in the arm.

"Would the winners of the treasure hunt please step up here," Mayor Rupert Rose went on.

Captain Roger Redbeard stepped onto the floor of the Town Chambers with Ellie and Sniffle. The council members gasped. The town clerk said something in the mayor's ear.

The mayor blinked again. "There seems to be some mistake! These children found Baby Face Ging's treasure. They are not the winners of the treasure hunt!" he said.

"Ahhhh!" said all the council members together.

The mayor pulled out the brown suitcase Roger had found. "Of course, these old English bank notes aren't worth anything now. You can have them all back. But we'd like to give you a token of the town's thanks!"

He pushed a chest at Roger and turned to the town clerk. "Now," he said with a smile, "where's my Ruby Rose, and where are the real winners of the treasure hunt?"

The Pitt Street Pirates were led out of the Town Chambers in a hurry.

It was hot outside in the street. "Open the chest, Captain Roger," Sniffle said.

Roger opened it and looked inside. Ellie took something out of the chest.

"What is it? Gold? Silver? Airplane tickets to Hawaii?" asked Sniffle.

Roger shook his head. Ellie held up a sheet of paper and read out loud.

> The Town Council wishes to express
> its thanks to Roger Redwood and friends
> for finding the Ging Gang goodies.
>
> Signed
> Rupert Rose (Mayor)

"They didn't even get my name right," Roger said as they walked back to Pitt Street.

"We found 1,000 old English pound notes, and they aren't worth a penny!" said Roger with a sigh.

"Will we build another *Titanic*?" Sniffle asked Roger.

Roger said nothing.

"Cheer up," Ellie said. "It could be worse."

Roger looked at her.

"How?" asked Roger. "I'm a pirate who never stole anything. The treasure I found is not worth a penny. I'm a loser. How could it be worse?"

"You could be Ruby Rose!" Ellie grinned.

A tricycle with gold and silver trim came around the corner on just two of its three wheels. Ruby Rose was pedaling like crazy.

"Help! Oh! Help!" she cried. "They want to kill me!"

"What's the matter, Ruby?" Ellie asked as if she didn't know.

"The country club kids have worked all day to follow the clues. They went nuts when they had to wade across the Pitt Street Park lake in their best clothes." Ruby gasped and looked behind her in panic.

"It would be worth it to find the treasure," said Roger.

"Yes! But when they got across the lake, the clue was gone! And they blame me!" Ruby wailed.

"How did anyone find the treasure if they never found the last clue?" asked Ellie.

"Officer Ello told them, but they're still mad at me," Ruby replied.

"She's here!" a voice called out.

A group of wet, muddy, angry rich kids came rushing around the corner.

They started to yell at Ruby Rose.

"Wahhhh!" she sobbed. "They say they're going to throw me in the lake!"

Roger smiled. It was the first time he'd smiled in an hour.

Ruby pedaled away as fast as she could.

The angry country club kids vanished around the corner after Ruby. Roger Redbeard was rolling around on the ground, laughing. Even Sniffle got the joke.

Ellie held up a grubby slip of paper with the last clue on it. "I think this is what got lost!" She was laughing, too. "Hey, Captain! Who said we couldn't rob the rich?"

"Robbing is wrong!" a shaky old voice said from inside the store. They were standing by the dusty windows of Mr. Clark's store, and it was the old store owner who had spoken.

The old man came to the door. "What have you got there?" he asked.

Roger showed him what was in the brown case. "Old English money," he said with a sigh. "Not worth a cent!"

Mr. Clark looked in the box and shook his head. "Don't be silly, boy! People collect old notes like those. They may not be worth a dollar each, but they are worth something!"

"How much?" Sniffle asked.

"A quarter at least," the man said. "I'll give you that much for them."

Roger looked at Ellie, and she nodded. "A quarter's better than nothing," she said.

The old man took the case and went back into the gloomy store.

Mr. Clark came out five minutes later with a fat bundle of money. "Here you are. There were 1,000 notes in there, so here's 250 dollars!"

Roger could hardly speak. "I thought you said one quarter!"

"One quarter for each paper note — 1,000 notes — 250 dollars!" the old man said with a smile and then went back into the store.

The three pirates dreamily walked down Pitt Street. It was sunset by the time they got home.

Roger sat on the warm doorstep and closed his eyes. The houses in the street turned into great galleons in his mind.

"We'll build that new galleon," he said. "We'll sail the seven seas and bring back Spanish gold!"

"What will you spend your share of the treasure on?" Ellie asked Sniffle.

"A bike," Sniffle said. "And you?"

"A new collar for Minnie," she said, stroking the pirate cat until it purred loudly. "Then there are one or two videos I want to watch," Ellie added, looking at Roger.

"Pirate movies?" he asked.

Ellie shook her head. "Romantic movies," she said shyly.

"Would you like to come and watch them with me, Roger?" She nudged him with her elbow.

Roger was looking across the street and seeing the great galleons in his mind. "I'll buy a new ship — a real sailing ship. It'll be the best on the seven seas."

"What'll you call it?" asked Ellie. "*The Fair Ellie?*"

Roger shook his head. "Noooo," he said. "The first ship led us to the treasure. It was a lucky ship for us. Yes! I'll call my new ship *Titanic Two.* I can't help thinking that's a lucky name for a ship!"

ABOUT THE AUTHOR

Terry Deary has authored more than
400 children's books. Some of his books have even
been made into cartoons. Terry is also a professional
actor and has performed in his own plays. He lives
in County Durham, England, United Kingdom.

NEW AND OLD MONEY

In England, the unit of money is called
a pound. Years ago, a pound was worth
240 pennies!

In 1971, the English government decided to make
things easier with a new pound. The new pound
equaled 100 pennies. Any paper money, or notes,
that had been printed before 1971 began to lose
value. That's why, when the Pitt Street Pirates found
a suitcase full of pound notes, the money was not
worth as much as they thought. The money was
buried by the Ging Gang before 1971.

GLOSSARY

galleon (GAL-ee-uhn)—a heavy ship used hundreds of years ago

gasp (GASP)—to breathe in quickly when you are surprised or shocked

mast (MAST)—a long pole on the deck of a ship; a mast usually holds a ship's sail.

mutter (MUH-tur)—to speak in a low voice

pound (POUND)—a unit of money in England; a paper bill, or note, can be worth one, five, ten, or 20 pounds.

rudder (RUH-dur)—a piece of metal or wood attached to the back of a boat that helps turn the boat

ruthless (ROOTH-liss)—cruel and mean

shrug (SHRUHG)—lifting the shoulders; people shrug to show they don't know or don't care about something.

token (TOH-ken)—a small gift to show that someone is thankful

DISCUSSION QUESTIONS

1. Ruby Rose demanded that Roger, Ellie, and Sniffle take her to the island in the lake. Even though they took her, Ruby was still mean to them. Why did she treat them so badly?

2. Mayor Rose gave Roger the treasure he found and a chest with a letter of thanks from the city as a reward for finding Baby Face Ging's loot. Why was Roger disappointed with this reward?

3. Roger was the captain of the ship, and Ellie was the first mate. Who do you think knew more about being a pirate? Why?

WRITING PROMPTS

1. Roger imagined that he was a pirate sailing the seven seas. If you could sail anywhere, where would you go? Write about the exciting things you would see?

2. How would the story be different if Roger's boat didn't sink? Write about where the pirates would have sailed next.

3. Roger found Baby Face Ging's missing money. Write about a time you found something that was missing. Did you return it to the person who owned it? Did that person give you a reward?

INTERNET SITES

Do you want to know more about subjects related to this book? Or are you interested in learning about other topics? Then check out FactHound, a fun, easy way to find Internet sites.

Our investigative staff has already sniffed out great sites for you!

Here's how to use FactHound:

1. Visit *www.facthound.com*

2. Select your grade level.

3. To learn more about subjects related to this book, type in the book's ISBN number: **1598890050**.

4. Click the **Fetch It** button.

FactHound will fetch the best Internet sites for you.